STIRRING THE SHEETS

by

Chad Lutzke

Cover painting by Robert Johnson
Cover design by Chad Lutzke

To become a patron, visit www.patreon.com/ChadLutzke

To sign up for my newsletter and be included in all future giveaways, visit www.chadlutzke.com

Dedicated to the old & alone.

And to Dallas Mayr/Jack Ketchum—a gracious man.

Foreword

I have never written a foreword or introduction or whatever this qualifies as. I'm not very good at non-fiction. I have trouble focusing and so the style becomes rambling and jumpy. But I'm going to try and hit all the right notes on why I love this man's work.

Chad and I "met" after a flash fiction contest. We both entered. I won first place and to hear him tell it, he was pissed a little and then he read and liked my story and messaged me. We hit it off. Now three years later, almost, and we chat daily. We bounce ideas off one another. We read stories for each other. We've written stuff together. If I'm honest, his early stories, while good, were basically Twilight Zone-ish twist-ending tales. Not terrible, but not on par with his newer stuff. Well written as though they were, I could feel something brewing underneath.

I'm not sure what the catalyst was for Chad, the gear-changing mechanism...something came bubbling through. His work began to ring with an honesty and a natural vibe that barely read as fiction. And a lot of the work was steeped in melancholy and sadness. These are areas I know a lot about. I've been mining that ore for a few years now and it isn't easy. You can find yourself in love with that darkness and not want to come back up. But it is also one of those emotions that is hardest to render with any honesty. You simply can't fake it. Let me bust out one of my metaphoric meanderings...

Sometimes the most comfortable thing we can wear is sadness. Shimmering buttons of pain and despair, tight, bright stitching of anguish and melancholy. It's always there waiting. Most just push that particular garment to the back of the rack and grab another garish and happy shirt to cloak themselves in. Others, those whom I find much easier to trust and like, slowly slide their arms into the sadness suit, feel the slightly scratchy woolen traumas and tragedies that have helped make it. Like a person collecting scars. That's really what we do, isn't it? We read and watch stories because what we really long for is confirmation. We really want to just be told that we aren't alone. We want to compare and measure and slap backs with a "But hey, we pulled through it, didn't we!?"

It has a way of worming its way in, like a chilly draft on a winter morning finding fingers and toes uncovered and lightly licking them icy. I'm friends with Chad, good friends. If we'd ever met in the real world, we'd be besties. But I have watched his work grow the last few years. While his stories were always fun and good, he really kicked into a higher gear with his 2016 novella,

Of Foster Homes & Flies. A novella that, for all intents and purposes, should not have worked. A story about a boy who keeps his dead mother hidden so as to not miss a spelling bee?! Sounds daft in a simple breakdown but let me tell you. That little book knocked me out. I cried no less than three times reading it. Three. It struck me how open and emotionally honest his style was, how he seemed to have freed himself from conventional tethers to pursue something heartfelt, and the results were astounding. He followed that one with Wallflower, a novella no less emotionally eviscerating but a lot more bleakly dark. A young man purposefully dives into heroin use and finds that it isn't as easy to swim back to the edge as he thought. Another gob smacker of a story.

Chad and I have been beta buddies for a while and I get to read damn near everything he writes before the rest of the world. I was lucky enough to read Stirring the Sheets when it was fresh and steaming from the oven. Tackling so many themes—loneliness, aging, guilt and grief—in a manner that is so realistic it made me shake my head. I didn't just read this thing, I watched it through the front window of my mind. So vivid and clear. Chad has another winner here. All I can do is hope that you read it and realize what a special writer we have in our midst. And that you'll note his name and read all he puts out, because between you, me and the doorknob...I don't think he's even warmed up yet.

~John Boden, author of *Jedi Summer &
Spungunion*

1/23/18

Prologue

While nervously watching the rearview mirror, the old man misjudges his turn, and the body thumps in the trunk against the impact of the curb.

"Sorry," he whispers. The corpse doesn't hear him.

He drives the car into his driveway and parks. A neighbor stands outside, finishing off a cigarette. The old man will have to wait to empty the trunk, but for now he'll take a peek. When the trunk opens, the familiar scent of formaldehyde and death hits him. The woman lies curled, her hair covering her mouth. The man frowns and brushes the hair from her face.

He closes the trunk. This isn't habit. It's spontaneous and desperate. It's a wound reopened, and a loneliness that stings like hell.

Chapter 1

Emmett is awake for ten minutes before opening his eyes. It's a morning ritual, lying there, reminiscing. Wishing. When he opens his eyes, the sun sheds light on his dismal life. Every damn day the sun reminds him.

He looks at the clock—6:39 a.m. He watches the glowing white digits slowly flip to 40–*click*–and thinks about how much Kate hated the old clock. She'd tell him he was a grumpy old man who hated change. She was right.

There's still an hour to kill before Emmett leaves for work, but it won't be spent on the couch. The sun sees to that. And it's never good to let his mind linger for too long where it shouldn't. He knows better. Emmett swings his legs off the couch, and the rug beneath tickles his bare feet. The rug is an old blue bathmat that doesn't belong there, but he likes the way it feels first thing in the morning. He wiggles his toes in the blue shag like it's warm sand on the beach. His socks lie in a ball next to the rug. He bends over, slowly, and retrieves them, the bones in his spine cracking—a reminder that seventy approaches and retirement should be considered.

A picture of an attractive woman in her sixties sits in a small wooden frame on the coffee table next to him—a half empty glass of water, a copy of *Let Go* by Francois Fenelon and a wristwatch surrounding it. Emmett kisses his middle and index fingers then presses them against the picture. "God bless you, Sweets."

He puts on his socks and his watch, then heads for the bathroom where his toothbrush sits waiting. For his age, Emmett's teeth are in exceptional shape, only a few molars gone. No crowns. No fillings. He flares his nostrils, checking for lengthy hairs. There are two. He pulls them and sneezes, reaches for his toothbrush, and stops. He hasn't eaten yet.

You've got a routine, old man. You think you'd know by now.

Emmett heads to the kitchen and grabs a pack of cigarettes sitting on the dining room table—Djarum cloves. He hasn't smoked in years but keeps one unlit in his mouth on the regular. Sometimes on bad days he'll even puff on it, inhaling deeply. But it's just air. Clove-scented air.

Emmett litters the table with a balanced breakfast—plain toast, eggs with hot sauce, OJ, and a bowl of Grape Nuts covered in honey. He's surprised at his appetite. Alarmed that he has one at all, particularly in the mornings. The mornings are the hardest to get through. Those first few hours reminding him that his wife of forty-nine years is gone. That her pillow will always be empty. No greeting arms and a smile to come home to. The best he can do is spray the sheets with her perfume, and pretend.

Until morning kicks his ass again.

Emmett finishes his eggs and toast, paces the house with the bowl of Grape Nuts, and stares out the bay window. He sees Julian across the street sitting on the trunk of his car, talking with friends.

Asshole.

Forty years ago, when Emmett bought the house, the neighbors were quiet and kind—one of many things that convinced him and Kate to live here. But it's different now. There are a few rotten eggs stinking up the place.

A grumpy old man who hates change.

Emmett finishes his cereal, downs his juice, then takes a long shower. He waits again to brush his teeth. Toothpaste and OJ don't mix. After his shower, Emmett sets out his clothes for work, carefully at the end of his bed: A plain white T-shirt to wear over a long-sleeved thermal, and a pair of blue Dickies. The attire of a factory worker, not someone forty years deep in the funeral home business. But it's comfortable. And familiar.

Emmett's bed hasn't been made in a year. Not since Kate died. The last impression her body made remains pressed—though barely—into the sheets, her pillow dented in the center. Emmett is careful not to disturb the linen memory when getting dressed. Before leaving the room, he bends over Kate's pillow and inhales. The smell of strawberry-scented shampoo has long been gone. The inhalation is a lost hope turned habit. Emmett looks at the pillow, pictures Kate snuggled in the sheets—her long, dark hair draped over the pillow in thick, shiny strands. Her hand tucked between her knees and the other under the pillow. He grits his teeth and fights back tears, takes a deep breath, and shuts the door.

Not wanting to be in the house alone any

longer than he has to, Emmett rushes toward the door. Passing by the coffee table where Kate's picture sits, he blows it a kiss, then leaves, locking the door behind him.

Oh, hell. My teeth.

He considers heading back in for a quick brush, decides against it. *What good are pearly whites if you've got no one to smile for?*

Emmett's Lincoln is backed up to the garage. It's a habit, backing up—using the work van to pick up and deliver bodies. The Lincoln has a sticker on the trunk that reads "Black Flag." Something Julian snuck on there. It's been there for months. Emmett doesn't feel like playing games with the kid, so he leaves it. And somehow the sticker seems appropriate. Whatever the hell it means.

"What's up, geezer?" Julian yells from across the street.

Without looking at the boy, Emmett raises

his middle finger. The arthritis tries to hinder the act, but Emmett doesn't let it. His finger stiffens, straight and prideful. It feels good, despite the pain.

Julian and his friends laugh. "And a good morning to you too, Mr. Irving."

As Emmett drives by Julian and his hooligan friends, Rosemary Dabicci is outside, flagging him down. If it were warmer, no doubt she'd be sporting a sundress, maybe one of those little hats, too. But spring isn't quite through with Candlewood Grove, California. And so, a pair of slacks and a blouse will do. Pastel colors, of course. Always pastel.

Emmett rolls down the window and pulls in front of Rosemary's house. "Good morning, little lady."

Rosemary walks around to the driver's side. "Oh, Emmett. I know you're a stubborn ole' mule when it comes to receiving, but…" Rosemary hands Emmett a plate covered in plastic wrap. "I've got these brownies here. They're butterscotch."

Emmett's favorite. He loves the gesture, but it makes him feel funny eating another woman's cooking, baking or otherwise. Like he's cheating on Kate somehow.

Kate's dead, old man. And change is gonna come whether you like it or not.

"That's awfully nice of you, Rose. How can I say no to that?" Emmett takes the plate, sets it on the passenger seat.

"Off to work?"

"Yes, ma'am. For the next seven hours."

"I don't know how you do it, dear. All that death. All those poor families breakin' down like that, weepin' their worst."

"I like to think of it as serving, Rose. Me providing a service that not just anybody can do. Something that's well needed."

18

"Oh, I think I'd lose sleep, all those bodies...decayin' and smellin'."

"Yeah, the smell gets ya at first. But the bodies are at peace, vessels I help appropriate for their loved ones left behind. A service." Emmett smiles.

"You're a sweetheart of a man, Emmett Irving."

Rosemary and Emmett both pick up on Julian's chatter, which is spoken purposely loud enough for them to hear. "...Is it widow or widower? I get the two mixed up."

"You shoo on outta here, Emmett. Don't let me stop you from serving." Rosemary attempts to draw attention away from Julian and his friends and offers a wide smile, crow's feet spreading to her temples. It's a beautiful smile. Full of love to give.

Kate's dead, old man. It's okay to move on.

***

It's a ten-minute drive to Griffin Gardens Funeral Home. Ten minutes spent humming along to Dave Brubeck—a clove cigarette in his mouth, butterscotch in his nose, and guilt in his gut.

Chapter 2

Except for the work van, Griffin Gardens' parking lot is empty. Emmett parks in the same space he has for forty years and grabs the plate of brownies. Trees shade the area now, but he recalls in his younger years taking lunches in his car under the hot sun, the vinyl seats cooking his thighs. The trees seem to have grown with him, making sure his old, sagging skin is kept cool during lunch.

Griffin Funeral Home, a family owned business that had only been established ten years prior to Emmett's employment. As a late teen just out of high school, Emmett cared for the exterior--mowed the lawn, raked leaves, trimmed a few bushes, and later developed an eye for landscaping. By the end of his second year there, the building was surrounded by vibrant, lush grass and an impressive array of foliage, slate stones, and topiary—something he took great pride in. That's when they changed the name to Griffin Gardens. Because of Emmett and his green-scaping thumb.

During those few years, he developed a friendship with the men inside and an interest in the science of death and process of bringing the dead to a visually acceptable state by way of embalming, makeup, simple procedures, and a slew of chemicals found on the shelves lining the basement. Emmett became an unofficial assistant, and by his third year there he'd enrolled in mortician school paid for by Mr. Jonathan Griffin Jr. himself.

Grateful for every day there, Emmett has called in exactly twice in four decades. And one of those times was to spend the day with a grieving widow who'd threatened to throw herself off her own roof. He sat on that hot roof for three hours, consoling, laughing, and crying with the woman. She lived another year until joining her husband, died in her sleep. Sometimes the elderly do that, follow one another into the afterlife organically.

Had it not been for a third Jonathan Griffin, no doubt Emmett would have been handed the business—keys, deed, bodies and all. But he wouldn't have taken it. Matter of fact he'd already been offered a higher position working upstairs with the public. And while he'd fill in when needed, he preferred the more physically demanding work over consoling and directing those who'd lost someone. His forte was the magic behind the curtain. The little things the mourning took for granted, hiding the ugly and the foul and bringing a glow to an otherwise dull pallor. Work that triggered compliments like "He still looks alive!" or "She hasn't looked this good in years" or even "About time he did something nice with his hair."

To Emmett it was never an art form but a way to provide for those who'd just been dealt more than they can handle, knowing he could somehow aid—even if just a little—in lessening the grief of those in need. He could use some of that himself right about now. And he supposes Rosemary was doing just that. She understood Emmett's situation—having lost her own spouse eight years earlier—and makes quite the effort to be the kind of friend she's always needed. But while the effort is appreciated, it isn't welcome. Not yet.

A year ain't too soon, old man. Kate would want you happy.

The bush in front of Emmett's parking spot has a discolored stem–a dead tooth in a sea of green. He gets out of the Lincoln, takes a jack knife from his pocket, and cuts out the eyesore. Griffin III hires a professional landscaping company now to keep up on Emmett's Eden, but they're not quite as meticulous as he is. It's something of a daily ritual, strolling through the parking lot and up the walk, looking for imperfections—a runaway stone, newly-sprouted weeds, or cigarette butts mingling with the mulch.

It's a Friday, Emmett's turn to open while Griffin III spends the morning at Wellshire Golf Course. Emmett unlocks the back door, opens it. The scent of too many flowers welcomes him. He walks down a long cement ramp, turns, and heads into a small room with a desk and paneled walls, adorned with oil paintings of sunsets—the sun touching the ocean, the sun kissing mountain tops, the sun peeking from behind city buildings. He'd hung them up decades ago. Reminders that despite the drab basement and its occupants, there was a bright world upstairs full of life and light. Now the paintings fail at their job, overlooked and collecting dust. No painting, no matter how big and bright the sun, ever fools him into thinking his life is something it's not.

Emmett hangs his keys on a small hook under one of the sunscapes, then heads into the next room where two stainless steel tables are set apart like twin beds for a couple in the 50s. *I Love Lucy* came to mind the first time Emmett saw the setup, a lifetime ago. Now it's just two workspaces to maneuver around, like pool tables in a bar spaced enough apart for a couple of people to dress the dead.

You rack 'em. I'll break 'em, Griffin Jr. used to say when directing Emmett to get a body from the cooler and onto one of the tables. Griffin would then prep, embalm, and dress the corpse while Emmett stood by, watching and learning.

Emmett feeds the CD player John Coltrane's *Stardust* and lights a stick of incense— Nag Champa. He burns it only at work. Kate hated the smell. She preferred the flowery scents— lilacs, gardenias, jasmine, roses. All of which filled the parlor upstairs. A permanent scent fixed into the carpeting and wallpaper.

Emmett grabs a pair of rubber gloves and an apron, puts them on. He and Kate used to joke about them both wearing aprons every day—him at work while embalming, her at home baking or preparing that evening's dinner. Every meal she made was his favorite. He couldn't pick just one: Roast beef with carrots and potatoes, chicken curry with broccoli, pork chops and rice and a side of fresh applesauce. Even her pancakes were the best he's ever had. He suspected she used a bit of cinnamon in them, maybe some vanilla. But he never asked. Now he wishes he had. Rosemary's brownies would be the closest thing to a home-cooked meal he's had in a year. He peeks in the office, glances at the brownies sitting on the desk.

Maybe later.

He leaves the prep room and heads for the cooler—a large, refrigerated room where the bodies are held until ready. While most funeral homes had updated refrigeration units with individual doors, Griffin stuck with the walk-in. The Griffins never saw a reason to upgrade something that worked perfectly fine, particularly when competing with other homes in the business. Any money spent for upgrades—except for the purchase of a newer oven—went to the parlors, making sure all decor and color was kept era appropriate and clean.

A note is stuck on the cooler door. It's from Chet, the on-call guy. The note reads: *Had a pickup last night. Priority. Tags are marked, file on desk.* Emmett opens the door, and the chilled air hits him. For a moment, the air gives no hint of death. It's crisp, almost pleasant. But soon is followed by the creeping scent of clay-like flesh, frozen faces, and pudding blood. A stench as familiar to Emmett as manure to a farmhand.

The cold room, about the size of a large

bedroom, has shelves that line the far wall. More shelves than they'll ever need. Two bodies lie supine next to one another, each covered with sheets, their feet exposed, their toes tagged. Each tag has its own colored sticker—one blue, one green. Emmett walks to the body tagged green and reads the tag. He looks at the head of the sheet. Thinned, wispy hair pokes out from under it—an elderly person. If it's a woman, any breasts she once had are now empty flaps pooled on her chest or nestled in the pit of her arms. He thinks of Kate's breasts. Though age had sagged her skin, loosened it, not a day went by where she couldn't turn him on. The way she kept herself. While age does its best to crush the spirits of the maturing, confidence is the best weapon against it. And Kate had heaps of it.

Emmett pulls a gurney from along the wall and wheels it over to the green-tagged body, adjusts the height of the gurney, lines it up to the shelf. He sizes up the body, then looks over at the pulley system. His pride won't let him use it despite his aging back. Not yet. Maybe when he hits that seventy mark. He tugs at the cloth underneath the body and transfers it to the gurney. His back feels it, but not enough to ruin the day. Lord knows, sleeping on the couch has done more to his back in the past year than wrestling any corpse. He wheels the body out to the prep room, transfers it, then raises the end of the embalming table.

He heads back to the office and grabs the file marked with a green sticker, goes back to the prep room where he matches the tag's info with the demographics listed in the file, checks the whiteboard behind him to verify the same.

With Coltrane's saxophone keeping the mood tranquil, Emmett turns down the sheet. It's a woman. Her face is blue and frightened. In the first few years of Emmett's apprenticeship, it was the faces that bothered him most. The removal of the sheet unveiling unpredictable expressions and conditions, more than a few times jolting him. Before he'd worked at Griffin, he pictured death as it's portrayed in film—serene with closed lids, not gaping mouths and wild, staring eyes.

The woman's sunken mouth suggests she has no teeth. Emmett pulls back her lips to reveal only gums. He grabs a set of eye caps from the drawer and takes note they need to order more. He lifts the woman's eyelids, places the caps over her flattened orbits and covers them with the thin, wrinkled skin of her lid. The eyes stay closed. Serene.

Along the wall, an old metal cabinet with various drawers and cupboards houses much of the materials needed for Emmett's work. Meticulous care from Emmett's own hand has kept the metal unit from rusting and the paint from bubbling. He opens a cupboard and grabs everything needed to make the old, gray woman's mouth remain shut: Suture, needle, forceps, cotton, scissors, and a clear plastic shield riddled with small spikes.

Emmett loads the needle with suture thread and carefully drives the needle behind the woman's gums and under her tongue, where it pokes out through the bottom of her chin. He pulls the suture through, then begins to feed it back into the same hole in her chin. He squints his eyes, then grabs the bifocals from around his neck and puts them on, feeds the needle back through, angles it, then pokes it up in front of the gums.

The process reminds Emmett of watching his mother rock in her chair, an intricate needlepoint pattern on her lap that would come to life several hours later, then made into a pillow. But this was not an art form. This was closure—in more ways than one—and nothing more.

Emmett tugs at both ends of the suture in a

sawing motion as it cuts through the tissues inside, until resting firmly against bone. He then directs the needle up under the top lip against the gummed bone and out the woman's left nostril, fed through the septum, then down through the right nostril and into the mouth again where any thread will be hidden from view. Carefully, Emmett lifts the woman's chin and pulls the suture taut, clips it, then ties the ends together, leaving the jaw lifted and mouth closed. He tucks the thread inside the mouth. It doesn't exist now.

Emmett lifts the woman's top lip and runs his finger across her toothless gums, taking an educated guess of measurement. He then takes a small pair of scissors and trims a plastic mouth former before placing it in her mouth. It's a flawless fit. He perfected the skill years ago, rarely needing to retrieve the form to trim it further.

Still, deep pockets in the dead woman's

cheeks give her a gaunt appearance. Emmett opens her lips one last time, and using forceps, stuffs her cheeks with cotton. Already she appears happier, healthier. Though her flesh hides a multitude of foreign objects, the outside conveys the serenity one expects from a lifeless body.

The phone rings four times before Emmett de-gloves and reaches it. A light on the old green phone blinks, signifying line two. This is not a business call. This is Griffin III, or maybe Chet.

"Hello." There's a low drawl to Emmett's voice that reflects his age, and his emptiness.

"Good morning, Emmett. Anything come in last night?"

"Yeah, Chet brought one in at some point."

"You get started yet?"

"Just set the features."

"Is the rest something Chet could do?"

"Yeah, a straightforward job. What's on your mind?"

"Well, we've got a body over at the examiner's right now, and I'd rather you pick it up. Chet could use some people skills yet, and the sister is hanging around. It's a sensitive thing for the family...a suicide. And I think they'd feel more comfortable seeing a gentle heart like yourself handling it."

Emmett peeks into the prep room, as though checking on the corpse. Still there. Still serene.

"Sure thing. Chet on his way?"

"He is. When he gets there, give him a minute to ask a question or two, then head out."

"Not a problem, John."

"Emmett... how are you doing? It's been a while since I've asked...I'm sorry."

"You don't need to check up on me, John. God blessed me with another day."

Was it a blessing?

"I got my health, my job, and a belly full of food. What more do I need?"

There is a moment of uncomfortable silence. Both men know it's not that simple, and Emmett is fooling no one.

"You're a glowing example for the rest of us, Emmett."

"You just haven't seen me before I get my breakfast." Emmett tries smiling, looks down at the brownies, picks a walnut from one and tosses it in his mouth.

Griffin III chuckles, thanks Emmett for the help, and hangs up.

The nut is bittersweet. Before Chet shows up, Emmett takes a bite of one of the brownies. It's good. Real good. The idea that they could be better than Kate's own is heresy. Besides, they aren't. And for now, Emmett is comfortable with that lie.

Chapter 3

When Emmett arrives at the medical examiner's office, a woman is standing nearby. Her eyes and nose burn red with grief, a wet tissue crumpled in the palm of her hand. She watches as Emmett signs paperwork and loads the body into the van. Emmett has seen this before—loved ones following their dead as far as allowed. A send off, like seeing someone to the door.

Before closing the van, Emmett turns to the crying woman. "This is your sister?"

The woman's face tightens. She nods.

"I'm sorry." He walks to her, grabs her shoulder and squeezes. "Allow yourself this time to mourn...as long as it takes. Scream, break things, and wail until you're weak and hoarse. And then wail some more."

The woman sobs uncontrollably. Emmett strokes her arm and squeezes again. "For as long as it takes." It's advice Emmett gives but never uses. He cried plenty when Kate passed, but he set a limit. There was work to be done and he needed to move on, whether he was ready or not. Problem is, he hasn't moved on at all. Steering clear of another woman's food and not stirring the sheets are sure signs of that.

Emmett refrains from hugging the woman and walks away. He sits in the van, watching her. He wants to wait, make sure she's okay to drive but knows she's not going anywhere. Not until he does. Like a young couple on the phone, neither willing to hang up first. He pulls away and fights back his own tears as the woman shrinks in the rearview mirror. This is something new for him, empathy. Not that he was heartless before Kate died, but now he has a connection with mourners that wasn't there before: An experience beyond the death of a grandparent or an old friend getting along in years—expected deaths. He contemplates the ache the woman must feel as she deals with the loss of her sister to something as preventable as suicide, and all the questions that would forever remain unanswered. Emmett doesn't have questions for Kate. His questions are for God.

As Emmett turns the corner and loses sight of the woman, he's not sure which is worse: The unexpected death that cuts deep, taking you by surprise. Or the slow decay of life from illness. He sometimes selfishly wishes that Kate would have left by way of the latter. He would have been able to say goodbye, to see her through it. Not wonder if she was afraid and alone while burning in a fiery crash on the freeway.

As Emmett turned the corner back toward Griffin Gardens, a tear did fall.

Chapter 4

Chet is outside with a cigarette when Emmett pulls up. He stuffs it into the sand-filled ashtray near the door and helps Emmett unload the body.

"Hey, Em?" Only one person ever called him Em. Kate. And he isn't fond of anyone else using the name. "I got a question for you. I noticed you didn't use the needle injector but used sutures instead. Isn't that a bit...archaic?"

"No teeth."

Chet looks puzzled.

"You shoot the injector into receded gums like that and you're taking the risk of the wire ripping out. Nobody wants that."

Chet sighs. "I should have known that, Em. I'm Sorry."

"Hey, you're here to learn, Chet. Speaking of which, call me Emmett, not Em." Emmett said it as kindly as he could, with a pat on the back even.

"Hell, I'm sorry Emmett. Sutures for the edentulous, and no more Em." Chet taps the side of his head, like he's proving he means to retain what he's learned.

"So, are we to get started on this one?" Chet nods at the body as they pull it out of the van and onto the gurney.

"Not yet, cremation. She can be ashed as late as next week if need be. This really gobsmacked the family. They're not ready, and they never will be, so we need to help move them along, get this part of their lives over with."

"Car accident?"

"Suicide."

The word shuts Chet up. He stares at the bagged body like he's never seen one before. You could see a thousand thoughts fill his mind, with a million words to say but none of them fit. So, he just shakes his head and says, "Damn."

Emmett nods in agreement.

Silence is held between the two men as they wheel the body down the walk and into the building. Before they head through the office, Chet speaks up.

"Emmett, please tell me you brought that plate of brownies to share, because you're about to find one missing."

Emmett chuckles. "I'm sure you earned it."

They make their way through the office, the prep room, and to the cooler.

"I could use your help laying her out if you don't mind," Emmett says.

"It's what I'm here for, boss."

"Then we'll go give your work a once over."

Inside the cooler, they adjust the height of the gurney and Emmett unzips the bag. Unsure of how the woman died, Emmett prepares for a faceless mess, courtesy of a shotgun. Or waterlogged and bloated from slit wrists in a tub, soaking for hours—maybe days—until found. It's neither.

Startled, Emmett steps back.

"What is it, Em?" Chet has forgotten the Em rule already. Emmett doesn't notice. "Someone you know?"

Emmett steps forward, looks at the body closer. Her pale blue skin is the only sign the woman inside the bag is dead. Her auburn hair is long with thick curls, as though done for just the occasion. Traces of lipstick remain with small smears onto her chin, scars left behind by paramedics in their attempt to revive her.

While some kill themselves with a quick impulse of anger or sadness, not considering the mess they'll leave behind, this woman cared very much. Whether it was narcissism or genuine concern for those who would find her, it's hard to tell. But it's not the woman's beauty after death that has Emmett's heart racing, his stomach churning. It's the eerie resemblance of his late wife in her thirties.

"Emmett! Do you know her?"

Emmett looks for the small scar Kate had across her left brow from falling off a swing as a child. It isn't there.

It isn't there because this isn't Kate, old man.

"Mr. Irving?"

Emmett breaks his trance and locks wide eyes with Chet.

"I thought I did, Chet. For just a second there."

"But it's nobody you know?"

Emmett doesn't want to admit it, because for a moment it feels like he's seeing his love once more. Even if she isn't breathing. For a moment he wants to remember Kate like this, not blackened skin stretched across bone, empty eyes, and a skeletal smile. While Emmett never saw Kate in that condition, he's seen burned bodies. They all look the same. And that was Kate prior to burying her. But this, this is Kate ten years into their marriage. This is Kate healthy and happy.

No, this isn't Kate at all. This is the corpse of a woman who hated her life and ended it.

"No, I don't know her. Just a little startled is all. I think I'm gonna give this pulley a chance. Got to learn how it works one of these days. Get yourself some lunch and I'll tackle this one on my own."

"You sure? I'd be happy to help."

"Between you and me, I've had a rough few days and wouldn't mind bein' alone, Chet."

"You make sure and holler if you need me, Emmett."

"Help yourself to the brownies, and I'll catch you in the prep room."

With some hesitancy, Chet leaves. Emmett looks back at the woman's face, searches for the scar once more. Without checking the cause of death, he guesses an overdose on pills or carbon monoxide poisoning. He spends a good minute staring at her face. This is how Kate should have died. Peacefully, holding on to her beauty. Not charred and screaming.

Emmett looks at the lift. Despite telling Chet he'd be using it, he decides against it and wrestles the bagged body onto one of the shelves. He fights the urge to look again, to stare, then zips the bag and heads for the prep room where Chet is waiting.

For the next few minutes, Emmett goes over the prepped body of the elderly woman, but his mind is still back in the cooler. While Chet makes small talk, Emmett wonders if the young woman's hair smells like strawberries.

Chapter 5

Emmett sits on the front porch of his house, puffing an unlit Djarum. He notices Rosemary has planted marigolds again this year and wishes he liked the smell of flowers, but they remind him of work, and he'd rather not take work home with him.

Or would you?

Emmett cracks open *Let Go* by Fenelon, reads a page. When he'd started the book, he thought it had been for the grieving, for those letting go of loved ones. But it's not. It's a book of letters written by an archbishop to those within the court of King Louis XIV, letters in the form of spiritual pep talks. Emmett reads it anyway, mostly because he knows Kate would have. While she didn't care for televangelists—never trusted them—she loved a good book about faithful living.

Emmett makes a tuna sandwich for dinner with sliced pickle and a side of applesauce, then goes over a short list of chores he made for himself. The sandwich goes untouched, but he eats the pickle.

It's a warm evening so he swaps out the list for another he's made with outdoor chores and tends to those instead. While trimming the bushes along the porch, the smell of cat urine fills the air. It's Julian's cats, no doubt. His mother owns at least a few. And like an ironic challenge to confront, Julian walks out of his house and to the mailbox.

While Emmett revolves recent life decisions around whether or not Kate would approve, there are times when he allows himself to do the opposite of what her gentle heart would applaud. Confronting Julian is one of those things.

Emmett grips his shears and walks down the drive, makes eye contact with Julian.

"Julian." Emmett says it in a matter-of-fact tone, with a nod in his voice—a forced greeting.

"Hey, Mr. Irving. Got your hands in some bush tonight, eh? I'll bet it's been a while."

Emmett ignores the tasteless remark.

"I've asked you before to keep your cats inside, or at least away from my yard. They piss all up next to my house."

"First of all, Mr. Irving, they're not my cats, they're Mom's. I personally can't stand the little shits. And second, they're cats. They go where they please. Spray the bushes off with a hose or something...or set traps for all I care."

"Or I could rub your face in it." Emmett says it before thinking. He'd lose in a fight to Julian. He knows that. And it hurts his pride to ponder such a thing—getting tossed around by an eighteen-year-old punk. It hurts quite a bit. Still, he has his mouth. And if it manages to find him trouble one day, then at least he'll go down swinging. Even if those swings are mostly from his tongue.

Julian takes a few steps toward Emmett, and in a threatening pose, with rage-filled eyes, says: "Let's see you do that, geezer. That old piece of ass ain't around to stop you anymore."

Emmett has a moment of daydreaming—him punching Julian hard enough to knock out a tooth or two, then Emmett receiving the beating of his life. The kind of beating that would send him straight into the arms of Kate, and Julian behind bars. It's tempting, but Emmett does nothing outside of trade stares with the boy and call him an asshole, then walk away with tears in his eyes. It doesn't take much to threaten a cry anymore, but it has nothing to do with pride or with Julian. It has everything to do with being alone.

The chore list is nothing but a distraction to keep his mind off the woman at the funeral home. The distraction doesn't last long, and he finds himself in front of the television, staring through reruns of old sitcoms, paying no mind. Come 11:00 p.m., Emmett hits the lights. And from the comfort of the aging couch, he watches the bugs congregate under the streetlight outside until sleep finally comes, but only in waves.

Chapter 6

Emmett wakes exhausted. This particular morning is the hardest he's encountered since Kate's funeral. It feels like waking from a dream filled with fame and fortune, only to find the bills are still piled and no one knows your name. He had no dream he can recall and attributes his distress to seeing the dead woman the day before. It haunts him, tapping relentlessly into his psyche and has refreshed the entire grieving process, opening a wound that had barely begun to heal.

Emmett skips breakfast and goes to the garage, which is cluttered with tools, leftover fencing, paint cans, a lawnmower, and boxes of old clothes, magazines, and books he's been meaning to get rid of for years. He pulls two photo albums from a box marked "*memories*" and brings them inside. He sets a pillow on the floor next to Kate's side of the bed and goes through the albums. The photos are roughly forty years old. Emmett cries when flipping through the pages of picnics in parks and on the beach, and impromptu photo sessions he would spontaneously demand after declaring how beautiful Kate was in that moment and that it absolutely needed to be captured in a dozen different poses.

Emmett falls asleep on the floor with his head on the pillow, his arm around the glossy paper memories, and doesn't wake until early afternoon, with the harsh realization of his reality.

Skipping another meal, Emmett heads for Princeton Park, a place of solitude he and Kate would visit often, even through the winter months. Their bench near the pond is taken by a couple feeding geese so he finds another spot under the shade of an old maple tree, where he spends most of the afternoon in deep contemplation, until visited by Rosemary Dabicci.

"Well, it's nice to see you getting out,

Emmett."

"Afternoon, Rose." Emmett begins to stand.

"Oh, please. No need for chivalry at our age. Hold your seat."

Emmett stands anyway, then sits only after Rosemary has gotten comfortable. It's a slow process for her, with arthritis crippling her knees.

"The brownies were delicious, Rose. Thank you." It's not a lie. He did have one.

"That's nothing. Wait'll you try my pecan pie."

Emmett smiles at the remark, but with no intention of trying anymore baked goods.

"I saw you and Julian trading words earlier," Rosemary says. "Don't pay mind to that jackass. He'll get his."

"I ain't worried about him. I'll knock that kid silly he tries anything on me."

Judging by the smirk on Rosemary's face,

she knows better. "I see a young woman out in public baring half her ass, all tan, hair done up, and I can't help but get a little envious. I haven't turned a head since Carter sold peanuts. It's okay to grow old, Emmett."

There's a moment of silence between them, until Rosemary confronts Emmett with a look of concern.

"You holding up okay?"

"Me? I'm doing just fine. Spring is here, and I've got some plans for the yard that'll keep me nice and busy."

"Don't bullshit me, Emmett. I see you out there sitting on the porch, a cigarette dangling from your mouth, staring off as if there's nothing left here for you."

Emmett gives an embarrassed, tight-lipped grin. It's true.

"How you *really* doing?"

"Oh, I have my days. I suppose today would

be one of them." He pauses. "You know about the smokin' huh?"

Rosemary giggles. "You mean the lack thereof? Emmett Irving you don't smoke, but you sure like to pretend you do. But I get it."

"Yeah, it's my thing, I guess." Emmett says.

"You do whatever it takes, Emmett. Whatever it takes to get through this storm, you do it."

"Thanks, Rose. You're a good friend."

"That's all I'm tryin' to be. Now give me one of them smokes." Rose puts her hand out, palm face up.

Emmett pulls the pack of Djarum's from his shirt pocket and hands them to Rose. "I don't have a light," he says.

"Don't need one." Rose takes the pack. "*Cloves?*"

"They got a taste to 'em."

Rose takes one in her mouth, puffs on it. "They do." She inhales deeply. "Twenty-eight years I've been without."

"Thirty here."

"It was the kids kept me smokin'. Until I graduated to a glass of wine after their bedtime. You and Kate, you had some good years together, Emmett. Don't ever forget that. And I'd like to think she'd give you the third degree if she found out you were moping around on account of her."

Emmett considers it and agrees.

"Sometimes things aren't that easy, Rose."

"No, they're not. But it *has* been a year. And I do know that ache you're feeling is never really gonna go away. It'll just move to the side and become manageable, instead of calling the shots. But you don't need to feed it. And if puffing on these, or talking…or, hell, even lighting one of these up, helps, then do it. But don't live the life you've got left like *you're* the one who's dead."

The words sting. After a year of mourning, it's become habit, and not something he's ready to get rid of. There's comfort in the loneliness, somehow.

"What do you say we go and get a taco," Rosemary says.

"Sounds tempting, but I think I'll stick around here. Collect my thoughts."

"Take heart what I said, Emmett…and I'm right across the street if you need me."

"Thanks, Rose."

Rosemary holds up the clove cigarette. "I just may break down and light this after dinner." She winks and walks away.

Emmett looks out over the small pond. It's tranquil. Ducks float peacefully on the surface, their feet kicking frantically below. Just like Emmett. He and Kate used to feed the ducks bread until she found out it was bad for them, caused their feathers to stick out at odd angles. Sometimes they couldn't fly as a result. It broke Kate's heart to think she may have contributed to such a thing. So, when she found out, from that day forward, she'd bring duck pellets, cracked corn, and frozen peas to feed them. And if she saw someone offering the ducks bread, she'd give them a lecture about how bad it was, about the wings and the malnutrition. Then she'd offer them the food she brought.

"I miss you, Sweets." Emmett says under his breath, looks around, afraid he's been heard.

A young boy, couldn't be more than eight years old, stands near the edge of the pond trying hard to skip stones across the water, and failing. Emmett searches for a flat stone and joins him.

"Afternoon," Emmett says.

"Hi." The boy says it without looking up.

"Flat rocks work best...the flatter it is, the farther it goes."

The boy looks at the round stone in his hand.

"Try this one." Emmett hands the boy his stone. "And hold it on its side between your thumb and forefinger, like this. Then when you let go, throw sidearm, like this."

The boy holds it as instructed, then throws it at the pond. The stone skips three times before sinking. The resulting smile on his face is contagious.

"Wow! Thanks!"

"The key is the sidearm throw. You do it right and you could even skip a marble."

"Really?"

"Maybe not very far, but once or twice, I bet."

The boy finds another flat stone, skips it four times.

"There ya go, now you got it."

The boy looks up at Emmett. "I've seen you

here before."

"Yep. I come here from time to time…sit on the bench, people watch, feed the critters."

Hell, all you need is a sweater with a tweed flat cap and you'll fit the stereotype, old man.

"That sounds boring."

"Believe it or not, it can be the best part of my day."

"That's kinda sad." the boy says.

"Yeah, it kinda is, isn't it?"

"Is it 'cuz you're old?"

"Yeah, I suppose that's part of it."

"Hey, I gotta go. My friends are here." The boy runs off, yelling behind him. "Thanks for showing me!"

"You betcha!"

Emmett searches for a flat stone, throws it at the lake. The stone skips once and sinks.

"Getting old can go to hell," Emmett says, then begins the walk home.

Chapter 7

Julian is messing around in the trunk of his car when Emmett gets home. He fantasizes about pulling the trunk down on top of Julian's head. Not enough to kill him, just enough to knock him out, maybe piss his pants in front of his friends. The thought—though cruel—is somehow therapeutic.

The little prick.

Emmett still hasn't eaten but forces down some applesauce with cinnamon. He gets comfortable on the couch, reads the paper, and turns on the television. For the next two hours, Emmett watches back-to-back episodes of Rockford Files.

Since Kate has died, Emmett has admired Jim Rockford's situation and deemed it perfect under the circumstances. Living on the beach in an old trailer by himself, being hired as a private investigator—two-hundred dollars a day plus expenses—driving around in a gold Firebird with a wit that gets him pummeled from time to time. And at the end of the hour, black eye or not, he's helped someone get their life back on track, while his own is still in shambles.

More than once in the past year, Emmett has wanted to run away from this life, settle down where he's a stranger. No more bodies. No more cat piss and defiant youth. But he knows he'll never do it. It'd be the true test of letting go, of moving on. Something Emmett has no interest in. Not today. And probably not tomorrow.

Chapter 8

Emmett wakes from his nap with Rosemary's words on his mind:

"You do whatever it takes, Emmett."

The reopened wound shows no sign of closing. The decades spent with his wife drown out every other thought in Emmett's mind. A montage of him and his love together, animated photos with the soundtrack of laughter, summer breezes, and sensual moans. One summer in particular lingers longer than the rest. In their early twenties they had both quit their jobs, collected their checks, and traveled north along the shore and into Oregon where they lived on the beach in tents, cooking by fire. It was spontaneous and freeing, and sharing those days with Kate bonded them. At the time, their decision was frowned upon by friends and family. But the lessons learned and the experience shared helped shape them, solidifying their marriage like no other. As fall approached, the two came back to Candlewood Grove not only as new people but as one, inseparably fused. Life after that summer was normal. No more spontaneous leaps into the unknown. It wasn't needed. They'd found themselves, and each other. Even now, the sound of ocean waves takes Emmett back to that summer.

Emmett rises from the couch, runs his feet through the blue shag rug.

Like sand.

He grabs the picture of Kate from the coffee table and heads out the door, driving west toward the ocean.

Chapter 9

Once on the freeway, Emmett spots a hitchhiker—a teenaged girl with a backpack and bedroll. He has no reservations about picking her up. Better him than some madman out looking for trouble. It's the first time Emmett can remember riding in a car with a female who wasn't Kate or his own mother, excluding the dead, of course. It feels strange, but there's no guilt. He's a temporary father figure, looking out for a naive girl far from home. She's heading for Ventura to stay with cousins. Emmett tells her he can get her maybe twenty or thirty minutes closer but that's it. For the next half hour, they talk literature, going over their favorites. The girl is well read and has a lot to say about books that others deem classics, mainly disdain for them, specifically *The Catcher in the Rye,* calling it overrated trash. On that particular read, Emmett agrees. But on the rest, he chalks it up to her youth and assumes her opinions will change with age. After all, what young lady has ever read *The Old Man and the Sea* and taken a quick liking to it?

Before turning toward the beach, Emmett drops the girl off at a gas station and gives her twenty dollars for food and something to drink. She's thankful and gives Emmett the name of a book to read, tells him he'll enjoy it, that it'll make him feel young again. He takes note and drives away.

Ten minutes later he reaches the ocean. The beach is empty and quiet. He builds a small fire and sits naked in the sand next to the picture of Kate, propped to face the setting sun.

Emmett reflects. No. Emmett meditates, as the ocean waves roll—liquid thunder. In this moment, Kate is with him. She's not a charred corpse, car and clothing melted onto crisp, black flesh. She's a beautiful smiling woman with skin like silk and eyes like stars that hold the power to seduce and speak a thousand words that all say she loves him, and will forever.

When Emmett opens his eyes, a cool breeze has raised the hair on his arms and shriveled his scrotum. The fire has died, and the sun is gone.

Whatever it takes, Emmett.

It's late on a Saturday night. No one is at Griffin Gardens. No one alive. Just two corpses, one of which could pass for his late wife's double. Emmett drives to the funeral home, his conscience screaming the whole way.

Chapter 10

Griffin Gardens is beautifully lit at night. A combination of both Emmett's vision and the landscaping company that carried it through. Apparently, it also sets a romantic mood for some, as more than once Emmett has shooed away couples laid out on the lawn under the trees, heavily necking.

The funeral home is usually empty by 7:00 or 8:00, except for the rare drop-off by those on call. It's eleven.

While Emmett walks toward the door, he tells himself he's going inside to check on things, maybe grab what's left of the brownies. He pretends he never backed the Lincoln up near the rear entrance.

Emmett goes inside, heads for the office where he checks for messages on the phone and notes on the desk. There are none. Three of the eight brownies remain under the plastic wrap. He doesn't even consider them but heads for the cooler.

What are you doing, Emmett? Leave the woman be. She didn't off herself so some dirty old man can gawk at her corpse.

"It ain't like that." Emmett says, to no one but himself. The sound of his own voice is a startling gunshot.

He enters the cooler and walks to the shelves, unzips the bag holding the young woman. It's like seeing her for the first time, like he doesn't trust what he'd already seen, and now it's been verified. Once again, his eyes wander to her brow, looking for the scar. He wonders about her eye color. Kate had brown eyes.

Emmett knows there's no sense in looking but does anyway. He lifts the lid of an eye. It's milky white with a slight blue hue that accompanies dead eyes, but under it all he swears there's a shade of brown. When he lets go of the lid, he does it gently and lets his hand trace the outline of the woman's face. Flashes of dates ending with long kisses goodnight race through Emmett's mind, and on his wedding day when he lifted Kate's veil oh so gently and brushed away her hair with his thumbs, grabbing her face in his hands and sealing the deal for a lifetime.

When Emmett snaps back to reality, the dull black bag is glistening under the florescent light with tears. Emmett wipes his face and whispers "Just for tonight," then zips the bag and reaches for the gurney.

Chapter 11

While no request for embalming was made by the family, Emmett takes the liberty of performing several procedures on the body that would otherwise not be done.

This is for him.

Two slits are made in the woman's pale skin, one in her thigh severing the femoral artery and another in the carotid, near her collarbone. A tube pushes a cocktail of chemicals specifically mixed for the corpse—all made for preservation—through the body, forcing the blood out onto the table where it drains. Emmett massages the woman's skin, allowing the fluid to go where needed. Her eyes have been capped and makeup will be applied after, but not until everything is washed and disinfected.

As the fluids fill the corpse, Emmett continues to massage the skin. The flesh is cold and clay-like, but a pink hue has replaced the jaundice tinge.

Once the procedure is complete, Emmett ties off the arteries and sutures the incisions made, applying a generous amount of sealing powder to ensure no leakage. A quick run through of the organs with a large, metal rod aspirates any trapped blood, then a drying fluid is injected. Through it all, Emmett never removes the woman's gown, nor does he peek at her breasts, checking to see if her areolas hold the same coral tone as Kate's. Instead, he is a gentlemen, has always considered himself one. When he met Kate, she was a virgin. He would have been too if it weren't for a mutually curious encounter he'd had with a neighbor girl one summer, the two of them in a fort he'd made with friends. The encounter lasted all of ten seconds. No ejaculation, just lightning quick penetration—once in, once out—enough for a quick change of minds for the both of them, a passionless and horrifying experience full of shame. Emmett waited as long as it took with Kate, not once pressuring her or even mentioning it. There was never any hurry. She was special to him, and he knew he had a lifetime. As short as it became.

To prevent seepage and a trail of fluids from here to his car, Emmett slides a pair of plastic underwear on the woman's legs and pulls them up under the hospital gown, being careful not to expose her privates. The body is then disinfected, and moisturizer is applied to the face and hands.

The body has been through the process of preservation, as well as methods utilized to bring the corpse to a state of peaceful beauty. Emmett wheels the body out to his car.

Chapter 12

Nervously watching the rearview mirror, rather than the road ahead, Emmett misjudges his turn and the body thumps in the trunk against the impact of the curb.

"Sorry," he whispers.

He backs into his driveway and parks. A neighbor stands outside, finishing off a cigarette. Emmett will have to wait to empty the trunk, but for now he takes a peek inside. The woman lies with legs bent, hair covering her mouth. Emmett frowns and brushes the hair from her face.

The neighbor is Dallas Doud. He'll be no problem. Dallas keeps to himself, is a good guy—maybe smokes too much. But he's not interested in anything Emmett is doing. He just waves, then gets back to his cigarette. Emmett shuts the trunk and heads inside. He pulls every blind, draws every shade, strips the couch of blankets and the coffee table of dishes. Kate would never allow such a mess. Emmett peeks out the window to see Dallas still in his cloud of smoke.

Once again, Emmett goes over the checklist in his mind: Prep room cleaned, utensils put away. Also, he'd stuffed the body bag with linens and set it on the shelf in the cooler in place of the body. Chet is new and did only what was told. There'd be no reason to retrieve a body from the cooler unless instructed by Emmett. And Griffin III hasn't touched a corpse in years—doesn't care much for that part of the job and tends only to the duties upstairs. The only person that has any business at all with the body is Emmett. But not this kind of business.

As Emmett creeps by the window, waiting for his neighbor to head inside, he questions his motives, his sanity. *This isn't me*, he repeats to himself. And it isn't. Emmett was a faithful husband, and a good friend. And while he doesn't necessarily consider himself a Christian, he figures if God *was* watching over him then He'd approve. Until now.

Dallas Doud crushes the cigarette into the brick of his house, tosses the butt in the garbage can, and goes inside. Emmett's stomach twists. There's a dead woman in the trunk and the couch has been cleared. God help him.

Chapter 13

Getting the woman into the trunk was easier than out of it.

Should have brought the gurney.

The garage is filled, completely unorganized and in no shape to hold his car. Emmett grabs a wool blanket that sits high on a metal shelf, lays it out behind the car. He struggles in the driveway as he lifts the woman's body up and out of the trunk, the popped trunk and shadow from the roof the only thing blocking any voyeur's view, while the streetlight threatens to reveal all.

Emmett sets the body gently on the blanket, his back protesting every move. He pulls the blanket into the garage and up to the steps leading into the house, then shuts the trunk and garage door. He grabs another blanket and rolls it up on the bottom step, where he rests the woman's head.

The position is unnatural, a reminder that there is no life here. This is a corpse in the first stages of decomposition, slowed only by chemicals. He sets her head back on the garage floor. She rests.

Emmett shakes a Djarum from the pack, unfolds an old Samsonite chair from the corner of the garage and puffs away at the clove cigarette. The clutter is a stressful reminder of Emmett's procrastination and the number of things he's avoided dealing with since the death of his wife. Hoarded tools, old books, and records. Items from hobbies long past: Empty canvases, paints, an easel. Planks, dowels, and scraps of wood for projects that will never be.

Sitting in the garage allows too much time to think, for rationale to take hold. He slips the smoke back into the pack and opens the door to the house. Carefully, he pulls the body up the two steps and across the kitchen's linoleum floor, around the corner and into the living room where he stops at the couch. He looks down over the woman. It's Kate sleeping, in a drunken slumber, at peace, young, and alive.

You can drag this body all over the house and down the block and it'll never be alive, old man. It'll never be Kate.

Emmett goes to the bedroom closet where Kate's clothes still hang: Dresses, pant suits, blouses, and slacks with an array of shoes that line the floor inside. He knows right away which outfit he'll choose. A white sundress accented with daisies. The daisies are subtle. The dress is quiet and clean. He had surprised Kate with it one year after having been away for the weekend to a convention. She was supposed to have gone with him, but her sister fell ill and so stayed behind to care for her. The convention was in Nevada. They had planned to make a week of it. Emmett returned three days later with the dress, a pair of earrings and a new bottle of perfume.

Inside the closet is a hook that holds several silk scarves in varying colors. Emmett grabs a yellow one, then heads for the bathroom to where Kate kept her fingernail polish. Everything in the bathroom is still where she left it. The shower with her shampoos and soaps, and the cabinet with her deodorant, toothbrush, and vitamins. Kate wasn't much of a pill taker. She practiced a holistic approach to illness and, with the exception of the occasional aspirin, took only natural remedies. Emmett would often joke that she would outlive him and marry a man half her age who *still* wouldn't be able to keep up with her.

Things like car accidents never came to mind, only disease and old age. Things that wanted nothing to do with Kate's arsenal of organic methods and healthy lifestyle. She was the real reason Emmett quit smoking. It's hard waking up next to the epitome of clean health when you reek of stale tobacco. And he'd felt guilty every time they kissed, that she was reminded of his blackening lungs with his ashtray mouth. So, with the idea that no woman should have to deal with that, he quit. But there was no way in hell he was letting go of red meat.

Emmett rummages through a wicker basket full of polish, mostly different shades of red, purple, and pink. Even a bottle of green, when Kate had felt particularly spunky one summer just a few years before turning sixty. She wore it once, decided it wasn't her, and went back to pinks, reds, and purples.

Emmett grabs a light pink and goes out to the living room, stops. The room is dimly lit. It helps the illusion. The lie. Lifeless legs stick out past the end of the couch. It's a morbid sight, like a crime scene. Emmett hurries to the body, pulls it onto the couch, rests the head comfortably on a pillow.

He keeps the gown intact. He's not

interested in seeing the woman naked. This isn't about sex. This is about hating yourself enough to go to extremes. It's about surviving, when all you want to do is wake up dead.

You do whatever it takes, Emmett...

Emmett pulls the dress over the head of the corpse, maneuvers it over the body, slowly, gently, as if there's danger in harming the dead woman. He tugs at the hem, flattens any wrinkles, then places the yellow scarf around her neck and drapes it across her chest—a bow on a freshly wrapped present.

Once he opens the polish and smells the acetate, Emmett realizes not once in 49 years had he painted his wife's nails, only the nails of the dead at work. He'd offered plenty of times to help her, insisting that with all the practice his skill was adequate enough. Kate would laugh and tell him to stick with the ladies who had no choice in the matter, and she'll take care of her own.

And you're still not painting Kate's nails, you sick old man.

Emmett spends the next several minutes painting the corpse's cold digits. While the polish dries, he paces the living room, puffing on a Djarum, his stomach empty and aching. His heart the same.

He parts the drapes over the bay window and scans everything touched by the streetlight. The road itself, Julian's house, a leaf that skips along the road, stops periodically, then continues its journey to nowhere. A dull white cat comes out from within the bushes across the street and stands in the middle of the road, watching Emmett. As though sensing it's not welcome—or that things inside aren't right—the cat turns back toward Julian's house and disappears into the shadows.

These days, Emmett despises the night. The quiet stillness it brings, a haunting reminder he's alone. The darkness hiding the captivating art that is earth and everything upon it. Be it the architecture of a beautiful home, the shine of a cherry red 1950 Mercury Coupe, or the vibrancy of lush greenery turned to nothing but blackened silhouettes once the sun sinks. If there was a way to shut the night off, to maintain the life the sunlight brings every hour of the day, Emmett would have done it a year ago. The night can be unbearable.

He shuts the drapes and faces the body on the couch. The dress, the polish, the scarf. It's Kate resting after church, a cat nap before an afternoon in the kitchen.

With a headful of thoughts Emmett longs to speak, he mumbles "miss you" to the corpse. He is uncomfortable with the words but needs them to form, to have life, to get out of his head and off from his tongue.

"I...I'm so sorry, Katie." The words seem to echo long after he says them. "I wish it were

me that...No, I don't. I could never do that to you.
I just wish...."

Emmett's face is wet with tears as he heads
to the bathroom, where he retrieves Kate's
shampoo, a book of matches, and a candle. He
takes them to the bedroom, lights the candle and
sets it on his nightstand.

Back into the living room, he moves to the
couch, removes the pillow from behind the
woman's head and replaces it with his lap. He
pushes the body upright and slides down the
couch, then slips his arm under the legs with his
other arm behind the neck, and lifts. He isn't
prepared for the weight and so drops back onto the
couch. He takes a deep breath, holds it, tries again.
Emmett's legs shake and threaten to give as he
struggles to stand with the body in his arms, then
heads for the bedroom—his biceps burning, his
back strained and cramping.

He stands over Kate's side of the bed, and

one last time studies the imprint in the pillow, the contour of the sheets—designs that the love of his life created the day she died. An intimate canvas, unique as a thumbprint.

He shuts his eyes and drops the corpse. The act is like jumping from a cliff, a point of no return. And the damage is done. The bed springs screech from the impact, the mattress caves then bounces back and flattens. The sheets ripple with a new design, formed by another. Emmett grabs the bed to stop from falling, and dry heaves.

Holding his barren stomach, he stares down at the body, the dim light from the candle falling across the bed as the newly-formed folds create fresh shadows. A still river of white linen crests licked by orange candlelight. The sight of the sheet's new design hurts, but with the slightest sense of relief.

Emmett squirts some of the shampoo on his hands, rubs them together. The scent reaches him and instantly Kate is in the room. He lightly caresses the dead woman's hair, leaving behind the essence of strawberries.

Whatever it takes to get through this storm…

He turns the body onto its side and climbs into bed fully clothed, shoes gripping his tired feet. Lying close to her, he caresses the corpse's hair. It's soft and recently washed and feels like Kate's. It *is* Kate's.

This isn't romance. This is intimacy. This is coping. And this is needed.

"I just wish you were here…"

He breathes deep into her neck, finds her rigid hand, and holds it tightly. Then drifts off to sleep.

Chapter 14

It's 2:00 a.m. when Emmett startles awake, holding close to the body, still gripping the stiff hand—fingers like the smooth branches of a cool autumn tree. The candle's flame casts a warm glow around the room with shadows upon the walls, darkening the bookshelf, blackening a picture of him and Kate together on their porch.

His few hours of sleep are filled with a dozen dreams, all spent with Kate—the time they'd gone to the fair where she'd gotten sick after riding the Ferris wheel—hoping she was pregnant, time spent on the water in kayaks they'd bought in their forties, shopping for groceries after renting their first apartment together, and making love in the park under a weeping willow at 3:00 a.m. The last dream triggering an erection. Once he is aware of it, Emmett jumps from the bed, pushing his stiff penis down in shame. He turns away from the corpse and stares at a picture of Kate sitting under a tree holding a glass of lemonade. Kate's smile is broad and full. There is contentment on her face, a twinkle in her eyes. Life.

The hell are you doing?

"I don't know."

Emmett's erection goes flaccid as he wakes from a delusion he never wanted to leave. With screams of frustration and grief, he pulls every picture of Kate from the wall, from the nightstand, blows out the candle and heads out of the room, shutting the door behind him. He grabs a beer from the fridge—the second from a six pack he bought months ago—and heads outside where he gazes at the stars while puffing heavily on a Djarum, wondering if God and Kate can forgive him.

Chapter 15

After an hour filled with tears and self condemnation, Emmett sleeps on the couch surrounded by pictures of his late wife. A night filled with continuous dreams, a reel of special moments from the past and some that never were, all with Kate. Only, in the dreams Kate is dead, Emmett lugging her around places she doesn't want to be, but with no means to express it. In his dreams, Kate looks different, smells different, like perfume sprayed over hot garbage—a lingering funk.

At 9:00 a.m., Emmett is stirred awake by a knock on the door. Immediately the realization hits him that there is a dead body in the house, in his room, on his bed. One that he stole from work and dressed in his wife's clothes, a corpse that he took the time to paint the nails of.

He springs from the couch, feeling for a

shameful erection that died hours ago. The knock repeats. It's a weak knock. It's neither determined nor angry. It's Rosemary. Through the small windows in the door, Emmett can make out a sun hat and guesses there's a pastel dress to match. It must be a nice day. With blurred eyes and mussed hair, Emmett answers the door.

"Good morning, Emmett." Rosemary, in her sundress, smiles. An extra ray of sunshine right there on the front porch. Any other day with any other person in any other predicament would take to her like she deserved.

"Since when do you sleep in?"

Emmett rubs the sleep from his eyes. "Stayed up a little too late, I guess."

"The world got you tossin' and turnin' with its evil ways?" Rosemary throws in a wink to lighten the tone.

"You could say that."

"You heading back to bed, or can I borrow

your ear?"

"Yeah, sure. Let me get my…" Emmett looks around, unsure of what he's looking for. He's stalling. It's an awkward moment.

"Well, it's not your shoes." Rosemary points down at Emmett's feet. "You always sleep in your shoes?"

The question is a good one. One that Emmett doesn't have an answer for, so he fakes a laugh and simply says no. Under the circumstances, it feels like an interrogation and his sweetheart of a neighbor is here to find out what a demented soul he really is.

"How about I get us some coffee?" Emmett says.

"I'd like that. Just as long as it's no trouble."

"None at all."

Emmett turns toward the kitchen, assuming Rosemary would take a seat on the porch. Instead, she walks into the house and stands, waiting at the door. She sees the impromptu shrine in the living room—a variety of framed pictures, all of Kate, circling the couch, on the floor, on the back of the couch itself, the coffee table, and a small one on the pillow.

Embarrassed, Emmett forces a tight-lipped smile filled with humiliation, like a young boy caught with pornography.

Rosemary's quick reply of "I think you should be a photographer. You've really got an eye for it," assures Emmett that she passes no judgment, that perhaps she understands.

"I've dabbled. Years ago I took a class, learned a thing or two and kept it at that. But I don't bother with it anymore."

"Well, that's a shame. You should keep at it."

No, what's a shame is what is on the other side of that wall, all done up like Kate.

"Well, thank you." Emmett makes his way to the kitchen, leery of leaving Rosemary to herself. "So, cream? Sugar?"

"Oh, whatever you're havin', long as it's not black. That's a bit much for this old gal."

"How's French vanilla sound?" Emmett yells from the kitchen, his hands shaking as he fumbles with the cupboard door.

"Perfect!"

"Okay, I'll bring it right out to the porch." It's the kindest way he can say get out of the house. She can't be in here. Not now.

"Gotchya...I can hear the robins calling me. I do love my birds." With that, Rosemary walks out of the house and sits in a chair on the porch.

Emmett opens the container of coffee to find there's enough for maybe half a cup. He searches the rest of the cupboards with the hope that he, or Kate, had placed some elsewhere. The search turns up nothing. It's for the best.

Emmett heads out to the porch and breaks the news to Rosemary. "Well, unless you want creamer with a pinch of instant, then I'm afraid I'm out." It feels like a lie, considering the more important dilemma Emmett is hiding.

"Then we're going to Greensmith, and I'm buying."

"Rose, I…"

"I'm sorry, Emmett but you're coming with. I know you have Sundays off, your lawn is mowed, you've got no hobbies...that you're practicing, anyway...and no other friends but me. So, I happen to know you aren't busy. And between you, me, and the birds, I could use a friend right now."

It's straightforward, and a little unlike Rosemary. She's the independent type who keeps her problems to herself, but something has broken her spirit and Emmett isn't in the habit of playing asshole. So, he shuts his mouth, locks the door behind him, and walks with Rosemary to Greensmith Emporium.

Chapter 16

Greensmith Emporium is part flower shop, part greenhouse, part coffee shop, with the seating fit snug into a lush courtyard surrounded by wrought iron fencing. It's quaint and surprisingly not as full as it deserves to be.

Rosemary orders a large blueberry muffin and a cup of coffee with cream and sugar, then invites Emmett to get anything he'd like.

"I guess I'll take the same." The truth is, Emmett's appetite remains absent, and while hunger pangs claw at his sunken gut, he'll be forcing down the muffin. Dishonesty of any sort––even pretending to be hungry—Emmett despises, but he fears confrontation if Rosemary senses something's not right. So, it's a white lie, a safeguard for the both of them. To protect Emmett from needing to speak more about dealing with loss and grieving and loneliness and nocturnal erections while in bed with a corpse, and Rosemary from having to hear about it.

Emmett looks around. There is one other person there, a heavyset man with a beard, typing away on a laptop that is dwarfed under his large hands. Emmett thinks of the picture he'd take if he still did that kind of thing. He still likes to pick out subjects and sceneries, sizing up their composition, but there's no more interest in actually capturing the moments. He does this silently while Rosemary sips her coffee, being careful not to make a clicking noise on the saucer as she sets the cup down.

"I suppose I ought to get to why I dragged you down here with sleep in your eyes."

Emmett smiles, listens, sips his coffee.

"I found this today when cleaning out the closet." Rosemary pushes an envelop across the small, round table between them. The envelope is blank, with the exception of the letter "M" written in cursive with red ink.

Emmett opens the envelope, pulls out a folded letter and reads it. The letter is addressed to "Madison" and is a formal "calling off" of an extramarital affair. The letter mentions a deep regret and a "newfound love" for the author's wife. It's signed Thomas Dabicci—Rosemary's late husband.

Emmett looks up from the letter at Rosemary, who sits staring into her cup. "I'm so sorry, Rose...you weren't aware of this, I take it."

"No, I was not."

Emmett struggles to find comforting words and tells her so. "I'm not sure what to say."

"Did *you* know about it?"

Emmett is surprised by the question. "Rose, I barely knew Tom."

"Would you have told me if you knew?"

"That's not a question I can answer. I suppose if I thought it was good for your marriage to know, then yes, I would have."

"Is there ever a good reason to not know when something like this is going on?" Rosemary grabs the note and waves it.

"Well, would you have wanted to know after Tom got sick?"

"No...I don't know."

"You had, what, three months together after Tom was diagnosed?"

"Eighty-one days."

"And how'd you spend those last days?"

"In love, like we were twenty."

"Well, as many questions as you may have now, I'm glad your last days together were spent the way they were, without that ugliness." Emmett points to the letter.

Rosemary looks relieved, as though Emmett has helped. She seems to contemplate what to say next, reviewing the words before letting them go.

"When are you gonna take your life back,

Emmett?"

"How do you mean?"

"I mean, I hate seeing you like this. You've put a pause on life. I can see it. That smile you give me, that you give people at work...that ain't real. I know you're broken inside, but lately I swear it's worse. And you look like hell."

You've no idea. Spooning a corpse by candlelight ain't exactly a man's scars healing...or is it?

"I don't know. Maybe I'm comfortable wallowing."

"Maybe. Or maybe you just don't know who you are without Kate. Fifty years is a long time."

"Yeah...maybe."

"I tell you what. I'm gonna go pay for our coffee and muffins, and then I'm going to the park. I've got a few things to consider myself, and the duck pond helps me untangle my thoughts.

While I imagine you'll sit here and continue to wallow, you're more than welcome to join me and untangle your own thoughts."

Emmett nods and smiles, but knows he's going nowhere but home.

Rosemary puts her hand on top of Emmett's. "Thanks for being my friend, Emmett. You've made this day bearable. You've got a head full of good advice behind all that sorrow."

"Thanks, Rose."

"No, thank *you*. Now if you'll excuse me, I've got a date with some ducks." Rosemary pays, then walks through Greensmith's courtyard and down the street. She was just dealt a harsh blow from beyond the grave with no way to confront it, yet she walks away with her head held high, a positive outlook intact. Emmett feels good to know she came to him, that someone needed him. He feels a little less alone in the world.

He thinks of Rosemary's husband and

wonders what drives a man to cheat on his wife and can't make sense of it. Once Emmett said his vows, he never so much as glanced at a bare breast for pleasure, whether on paper or in film. Kate was it.

He doesn't touch the blueberry muffin but orders another cup of coffee and sips on it long enough to remember there's a corpse in his bed, then leaves a tip and hurries home.

Chapter 17

Emmett spends the day close to the house, tending to the lawn—pulling weeds, trimming the bushes, raking dead grass. Late in the afternoon he manages to down a few sandwiches and a glass of milk.

As Emmett sits on the porch, a Djarum between his lips and a wish for darkness to hide the transport of the body inside, Julian walks out to his mailbox. Halfway there, he spots Emmett and slows his walk, bending forward as though holding a cane, mocking the elderly with an unstable shuffle. Emmett wants to salute the boy with another stiff finger, maybe a few harsh words, but he doesn't want to draw attention and so sits and gulps down the rest of his milk, daydreaming about broken noses and blackened eyes. Julian gets the mail, straightens his posture, and laughs while heading back inside.

A Blue Jay lands on the birdhouse in Emmett's yard. A birdhouse that Kate had built and painted bright colors. Before she died, Emmett promised to spray a protective enamel coat on it but never did. And now the paint is cracked by the weather, the color dulled by the sun.

The Blue Jay pecks away at the house, loud taps on the yellow walls. Each tap feels personal, and Emmett's instinct is to rise from his chair and chase the bird away, to stop it from further destroying Kate's hard work. Because it doesn't give a shit about his wife or the house she provided for the asshole bird. Instinct leads to action and Emmett scrambles toward the birdhouse, cursing at the creature to get the hell away. The boom of his voice triggers an epiphany, enlightenment. Being a grumpy old man toward juvenile delinquents is one thing, but chasing God's creatures across the lawn and stealing dead bodies is another. Death didn't just steal away his bride, it stole rationale, mental health, and hope. Not everything in this life is somehow connected to Kate or her death or what should have and could have been. That's loneliness and desperation. That's paranoia.

The rest of the day is spent killing time, wishing for the ugly dark, avoiding the bedroom, and praying the phone never rings—Griffin III on the other end in hysterics about a misplaced corpse.

In the evening, as Emmett sits on the porch reading the same page of a Louis L'Amour book over and over again—the words never staying long enough to be retained—Rosemary waves from her house. She makes no sound, doesn't say hello, just waves Emmett over. Emmett closes the book and walks across the street. Rosemary has a wide grin on her face, as though trying to keep from laughing. Next to her on the ground sits a small wicker basket covered with a kitchen towel patterned with fading flowers.

"You look like you're doing better than most," Emmett says.

"Well, you really helped me this morning, Emmett. And I figure I owe you one, so this here basket contains what I believe is the recipe that will brighten your day."

The words strike fear into Emmett. It never makes him feel good to turn down Rosemary's cooking, knowing she works so hard on it for no one but herself. And a friend too screwed up to enjoy it.

"What recipe is that?" Emmett humors her.

Rosemary pulls the towel from the basket to reveal nothing but four eggs.

Confused, but relieved there are no baked goods, Emmett says, "You gonna juggle those?"

Rosemary grabs two of the eggs, hands them to Emmett, her smile growing all the more.

"There's your target." Rosemary nods at Julian's car in the driveway next door. Its slick, black paint shimmering under the setting sun.

"You serious?" asks Emmett.

"I figure we've got just enough time to send all four of these off before asshat makes his way outside."

"You *are* serious."

"Emmett, we don't have but one life, and it isn't meant for moping and it isn't meant for getting stepped on. Damn near every day that little prick is out here causing some kind of trouble with somebody, and I don't like the kid anymore than you do. The problem is, I don't know if he's even old enough to take a fist from a grown man, or woman, without one of us going to jail. But I do know he's got a car he don't deserve. You can join me, or you can keep on hiding behind that frown of yours. I'm throwing on three...*One.*"

"In the daylight?"

"Hell yes...*Two!*"

Emmett looks down at the eggs, looks at Julian's car and decides this is either the dumbest thing he's done in thirty years—other than stealing a body—or it's the best thing he's been a part of all year.

"*Three!*"

Rosemary tosses an egg at the car. It hits the hubcap, a loud tinny smack. With giving no more thought about it, Emmett tosses one of his eggs, hitting the driver's side door. The alarm is triggered, filling the neighborhood with a frantic siren accented by blasts from the horn. Rosemary throws her other egg. It hits the top of the car, breaks open and leaves a slimy trail across the roof and into the yard. Emmett takes his time, aims with one eye squinted and whips the last egg, a major league pitch. It smashes against the window, spraying out—the window now a blurred mess of yellow goo and eggshell shrapnel.

Rosemary breaks into a laugh that is unexpectedly loud for such a petite woman. Emmett follows suit. It's a relief. And it's unfamiliar. He hasn't laughed in a year—the day before Kate was killed to be exact. Two squirrels had chased one of the neighbor cats back across the street and into a tree where the cat stood its ground and puffed up into an orange and white ball, hissing wildly. Just what Emmett had been wanting to do to Julian the past year, pose a threat and chase him away.

Julian tears out of his house and toward his car, the alarm ridiculously loud. He slows when he sees the egg. And then he sees Emmett and Rosemary—Rosemary choking back laughter, Emmett with a stern face.

Julian turns off the alarm. "You did this?"

"Nope. They went that way." Rosemary points down the street. "Couple of gangsters. Looks like you ticked *someone* off, kid."

Julian doesn't seem convinced. He looks at the basket on the ground, then at Emmett, who is burning holes through him—looks that don't kill but do great bodily harm, looks that maim the ego. Julian doesn't say a word. He looks as though he can't figure out what the hell just happened. It doesn't make much sense that a couple of old folks would do something like egg a car, but looking down the street there's no sign of anyone else. For now, Julian looks like the ass that he is, and so he takes to the hose and sprays off his car, using a towel and a toothbrush for the bits that are stuck in the cracks of the door and hubcap, while Rosemary and Emmett stand and talk and watch the show, reveling in it.

"Thanks, Rose. I'm not gonna lie. That felt good. *Real* good."

"You've got yourself a nice laugh, Emmett. It was good to hear."

It draws closer to dark, closer to when

Emmett can break his back over a rotting stiff and sneak it back into work. The thought of what lies ahead makes him weary. He thanks Rosemary once more and tells her he needs to go.

"You sure you won't stay for dinner? I got plenty enough for two. Made some meatloaf, scalloped potatoes, and these little cakes...can't remember what they're called. Supposed to be good...but I can't promise anything."

"You do love to tempt me, Rose. But I've got some stuff to deal with at work."

It's the first time he has turned her down when he really didn't want to. He wanted to stay, to get another laugh in before night casts its blinders on the world and shuts down the city.

Emmett enters his house and breathes in the death laid out in the next room—such a familiar smell. But one that should never be in his home.

Chapter 18

Before starting with the task ahead, Emmett eats a few saltines and brushes his teeth. The phone rings. It's not a sound he wants to hear while the body is still with him. He imagines a call from work, Griffin III declaring he knows what Emmett has done, telling him he's always known something wasn't quite right with him, that he's sick in the head and the police are on their way.

"I'm not sick...I'm dying inside."

Tell that to the police. They're pulling up now.

Before Emmett answers the phone, he peeks through the curtains. Black is hiding earth's beauty, lit only by the single streetlight. No police car in sight. Could they be parked down the street? Seconds from crashing through the bay window, in search of a stolen corpse?

This is paranoia.

"Hello?" Emmett says into the phone.

"Hey, Emmett. It's Chet. I hope I didn't wake you or anything, but it's pretty important."

Emmett swallows toothpaste that lingers at the back of his tongue.

"No...that's fine. What's going on?"

"It's this body here at the home. There's nothing there."

Emmett's mouth dries, his heart races, and a cold chill rushes through him—spider legs along his spine. He's still.

"Emmett?"

"Sorry, what do you mean there's nothing there?"

"Maybe you didn't get my message. I left one about an hour ago."

Emmett looks at the answering machine sitting on the end table. A red light blinks.

"No, sorry I didn't."

"Okay, well, basically, I picked up a body tonight...and...Emmett it's about half gone, waterlogged as all get-out. Washed up on the beach. They think it was dumped there but it looks like something's devoured half of it. And I gotta be honest, Emmett. This is way out of my league. I'm not even sure what the hell to do. I got him in the cooler now, but...I just don't know."

Emmett lets go of the breath he'd been holding. A weight lifted off from him. For now.

"Go ahead and leave it in the cooler, fill out the paperwork and leave the appropriate notes. I'll deal with it tomorrow." Emmett chuckles while he says it, mostly out of relief. "And you should probably come in tomorrow for this one....how about just after lunch? You can learn a thing or two."

"Thanks. I'll be there. Some days I'm not sure I'm cut out for this job, Emmett."

"We've all been there, Chet. You'll get it.

116

Just don't ever expect to forget everything you see. Sometimes work comes home with you whether you like it or not. But if it's any consolation at all, I think you're doing a fine job."

"Thanks, Emmett. That means a lot coming from you. I'll see you tomorrow."

Emmett plops onto the couch, looks at the pictures of Kate and thinks about what he'd just said about bringing work home with him. A fit of laughter builds inside that he doesn't let out, as though doing so would confirm insanity.

He'll give Chet another hour before he leaves the house. In the meantime, Emmett prepares to transport the body. He grabs the wool blanket, drapes it over his arm and stands outside the bedroom door, hesitating. On the other side of the door are two things he doesn't want to face:

Admittance, that at least for one evening, he lost his mind. The other is the end of Kate's art. The sheets now hold the shape of the husk of a stranger, a woman he'd never met. It was like letting a graffiti artist paint over the ceiling of the Sistine Chapel—an ugly reminder of a regrettable decision.

"Oh, hell." Emmett bursts through the door with the intent of grabbing the corpse, putting it on the blanket and dragging it out of the room. But he stops, and stares. The beauty that was there before has faded, whether it be from the progression of death itself or because the illusion is broken, is unclear. Like waking from a one-night stand and attempting to make sense of it all, reflecting on the thoughts the night before and how things seemed like a good idea while under the influence. Under the influence of what? Morbid desperation? Insanity?

The face was no longer Kate's doppelgänger, reflecting the beauty of her youth, but a sunken nightmare of stretched skin and poking bone. If only her hair would cover the hideous lie.

Emmett charges the bed and covers the corpse with the blanket, rocking it back and forth, cocooning the body in wool. He then tugs at the very sheet he's preserved for so long—the desecrated canvas—until the body crashes to the floor. Emmett pulls the body through the bedroom, the living room, the kitchen, and out into the garage—a reversal of last night's mistake. No. Heinous sin. Is it even forgivable? God may pardon him, and Kate have understanding, but can he forgive himself?

At 7:40 p.m., a peek through the garage window assures Emmett that the neighborhood is empty of peering eyes. No Julian. No Dallas feeding his habit. Rosemary's kitchen light is on, and her figure glides past the window. He's noticed she's often up late and wonders what she does to occupy her time. Continuous baking? Reading cookbooks? Floriculture? It occurs to

him he doesn't know much about her but wishes
he did.

Emmett opens the garage door, then the
trunk of the Lincoln. He wrestles the body in. His
atrophied muscles still weak from the day before
and not at all interested in helping. The task is
completed using adrenaline only.

The trunk is shut, and the house closed up.
Emmett doesn't recall the route he takes to work.
His mind is elsewhere. When he pulls into Griffin
Gardens, Chet is gone. He backs up to the funeral
home, unlocks the building and wheels a gurney
out to his car.

Exhausted, Emmett pulls the blanket-
wrapped body onto the gurney—the top half first,
then the bottom. There's an audible crack from his
back, and his knees give. Emmett holds tight to
the gurney to keep from falling. No time to rest or
recover, he rolls the body to the door and into the
building.

On the office desk are the notes from Chet and the file for the body in the cooler they reference. The plate that once held brownies sits next to it, now empty and peppered with crumbs. Emmett is glad to see they're eaten, that Rosemary's offering didn't go to waste.

The cooler is rank from the new corpse not yet chilled. The body bag is bunched high in the center, as if only a boulder of flesh lay inside. While Emmett would love to spare Chet the grief of messing with it, the truth is that's the only way the kid will learn—hands on experience. He'll have to endure.

Emmett wheels the gurney over to the bag stuffed with linens, unzips it. The thought of getting the woman's body back into the bag is troubling. He can end this all right now, rid the world of Kate's doppelgänger and turn it to ash. He has the papers, signed and in his possession, the identification disc on a chain around her wrist.

Why wait any longer to do what needs to be done?

Emmett pulls the linens from the body bag, sets the bag on the shelf with others that are empty, then wheels the body back out of the cooler and into the office where he grabs the woman's file and compares the ID numbers with those on the disc. He doesn't look at the name, only the numbers. He'd rather not know her name. He double checks the numbers and places the metal disc in his pocket.

He wheels the body down the hall and into the crematorium, where a giant silver oven sits in the middle of the room, a single door in the center with colored buttons and dials embedded in a panel on the side. Emmett grabs a flattened container made of cardboard and lays it out on a large hydraulic lift, then shimmies the corpse onto it. He starts to raise the cardboard walls, building a makeshift coffin around the body. He's never been good at this part, a reminder that he'd never make it as a carpenter.

When Emmett was younger, he would dream of building a small cabin on lakefront property for him and his wife somewhere in Northern California. As they grew older, the idea became less attractive for the both of them, especially after buying their house in Candlewood Grove. At the time, it was everything the two of them ever wanted. Everything but the lakefront.

He stops building the walls and instead rips them off, letting them fall to the ground. The body lies on a jagged sheet of cardboard wrapped in the wool blanket, the woman's face and Kate's dress exposed.

Emmett pushes a button on the lift, and it measures the weight of the body, a tool he doesn't need. His ability to judge proper settings on the oven without weighing in is something that can't be taught. It's decades of practice. He pushes another button, and the chamber door opens.

Emmett folds the sheet that once held the imprint of his wife's last night in their bed and sets it across the face of the woman. He cries as he pushes the body off from the lift and into the open mouth of the oven. The sound of cardboard against brick is disheartening. A sound that never bothered him until now. He takes the ID from his pocket and places it just inside the oven. Protocol.

Emmett leaves the safety door open and more buttons are pushed. An orange glow lights the inside of the chamber, heating Emmett's face, threatening to dry his tear-laden eyes. This feels like the goodbye that Emmett never got, as Kate's yellow dress splits with holes and shrinks into blackened strands.

"Kate! I love you!..."

Another flame kicks on. The heat is tremendous, and Emmett is forced to shut the oven door. The low hum of the oven fills his ears, a bass-like drone that is horrifically tedious.

"I love you, Kate!" The words are slurred, shouted through a face stretched with despair, a sadness that convulses the old man's body and sends him crashing to his knees.

This is Kate in her car, consumed by fire. This is Kate's end. Emmett prays to God she was unaware, that she was not conscious, clawing at the windows as the heat broke through her skin and boiled her blood, that upon impact with the tree it was already over.

"Kate, I need to move on, Sweets!" Emmett's vision blurs, swimming in salt. "Please understand…!" He screams above the groan of the flames, his face a flood of snot and tears, child-like cries that would crush and scar any who heard. "I'm dead inside!"

While the body turns to ash, Emmett remains on the floor. For an hour he sits, soaked in grief, a cleansing that stings as much as it heals. Every bit necessary. The hour is spent in reflection, of the past, of the present, of letting go not just of Kate but the sin against her.

When he rises—aching bones and puffy eyes—he's lighter. Decisions about moving on have been made. No more wallowing in despair. And there will be no baby steps. He will run into the arms of life and drown in its brilliance. In the light of the day, and in the darkest of nights, he will capture each thought and command its obedience to letting go and moving on...and on and on.

It's 9:00 p.m. Emmett opens the oven door and checks the remains—human sandcastles formed in white ash. He considers waiting for them to cool, then process them, but grows tired and tells himself Chet could use the practice. He shuts the door and leaves Griffin Gardens.

Chapter 19

Emmett strips the bed of the remaining fitted sheet and throws it in the garbage. There are more in the hall closet but he's not using them. They're covered in flowers. Yellow ones. He'll get new sheets tomorrow. But for the first time since Kate's passing, he will sleep on the bed, alone.

Emmett checks his answering machine and listens to Chet's message from earlier. Emmett is thankful for the last 40 years at Griffin's, the opportunities they've given him, a secure job with stable income, a hand with school, and a feeling like he belonged, like he was needed. But he's seen enough death. Tomorrow he'll put in his resignation and give them whatever time they need while Chet gets up to par.

After Emmett cleans up the pictures of Kate, a single one remains hanging on the wall in the living room, where it will stay. The rest are packed away in a tote where he'll have easy access to them. He'll never forget her, nor will he try, but a shrine that screams obsession is no longer welcome here.

Emmett parts the curtains and looks out along the street. Rosemary's kitchen light is on. She's still awake. Again, Emmett considers what she must do with her time and finds himself with an appetite, while contemplating the many baked goods fashioned in that kitchen.

Emmett grabs his Djarums and heads out the door. He walks across the street, and the streetlight settles on something in Julian's yard—a white pail with a washcloth draped over the side and a garden hose stretched out nearby—tools of labor necessary for some post-vandalism cleanup, mischief courtesy of a couple of old folks: A geezer and his friend. The sight triggers a grin.

As Emmett approaches Rosemary's house,

it smells of flowers and food—sweet and filling. Emmett rings the doorbell and listens. Moments later, the light steps of a petite woman in socks on a hardwood floor grow closer. The porch light turns on, and the silhouette of Rosemary's curled hair pokes up from the small windows in the door.

"Emmett?" The door opens. "Everything alright?"

"Evening, Rose. I don't suppose you've got some of that meatloaf left over, for a friend?"

Rosemary holds open the door, a wide smile, the crow's feet at her eyes reaching farther than usual. Emmett turns to shut the door behind him and catches a glimpse of his house down the road, the moon casts an inviting white-blue hue on his freshly mowed lawn, the sculpted bushes, and even the brightly colored birdhouse with its peeling paint.

The night hid nothing anymore.

To become a patron, visit www.patreon.com/ChadLutzke

To sign up for my newsletter and be included in all future giveaways, visit www.chadlutzke.com

Other books written by Chad Lutzke:

Get Of Foster Homes and Flies

A neglected 12-year-old boy does nothing to report the death of his mother in order to compete in a spelling bee. A tragic coming-of-age tale of horror and drama in the setting of a hot New Orleans summer.

"Original, touching coming of age."
  ~Jack Ketchum, author of The Girl Next Door

"...a cracking coming-of-age story and a gut punch of emotional horror. I cheered when I read the final sentence."
  ~ Richard Chizmar, co-author of Gwendy's Button Box

Get The Pale White

After being held against their will in a house used for trafficking, three girls plan their escape.

Alex: A hardened goth-punk who's convinced she's a vampire with a penchant for blood.

Stacia: A seventeen-year-old raised by an alcoholic mother, her fellow captives the only family she's ever truly had.

Kammie: The youngest of the three—a mute who finds solace in a houseplant.

But does life outside the house offer the freedom they'd envisioned? Or is it too late, the scars too deep? A coming-of-age tale of revenge and survival that explores a friendship and the desperate measures taken to ensure they stay united, held together by the scars that bind them.

Get Skullface Boy

"My name is Levi. I'm 16. I've got a skull for a face. And here's how shit went down."

Having never been outside the walls of Gramm Jones Foster Care Facility, sixteen-year-old Levi leaves in the middle of the night with an empty backpack and a newfound lust for life. A journey that leads him into the arms of delusional newlyweds, drunkards, polygamists, the dangerous, and the batshit crazy. His destination? Hermosa Beach, California where he's told there is another like him, with the face of a skull.

A coming-of-age road trip filled with surreal Lynch-ian encounters exploring the dark, the disturbing, and the lonely in a 1980s world—an epic venture for one disfigured boy struggling to find his place in the world.

"This is Huck lighting out for the territories, and kind of documenting an era for us on the way. Only--because it's now not then--he's got a skull face to deal with. As do we all."

~Stephen Graham Jones, author of The Only Good Indians and Mongrels

Get The Neon Owl: When the Shit Hits the Van

Jinx is a record-collecting, middle-aged minimalist whose dreams of becoming a detective are waylaid by love and laziness. But when he inherits his late aunt's rundown motel, The Neon Owl, his passion for investigative work reignites while he searches for answers as to who keeps shitting in the bushes. His findings lead to a full-blown murder mystery where he and new-found friend, Roddy, the elderly, one-legged handyman, set out to find the killer

.A crime noir-ish whodunnit rife with humor, grit, and ranch dressing.

"Terrific stuff from Chad Lutzke, who manages to take tired tropes and set them on fire with passion and originality."
~Joe R. Lansdale, Champion Mojo Storyteller

Get Wallflower

After an encounter with a homeless man, a high school graduate becomes obsessed with the idea of doing heroin, challenging himself to try it just once. A bleak tale of addiction, delusion, and flowers.

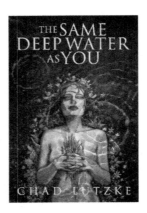

Get The Same Deep Water as You

Music, beer, skateboarding, and tragedy star in this coming-of-age lesson on love and lust and the line that divides them, as 19-year-old Jex experiences a life that meets River's Edge and Kids with Dazed & Confused—a parentless indie yarn with the dark heart Lutzke is known for.

Get Out Behind the Barn

The boys crept to the window and watched as Miss Maggie carried the long bundle into the barn, the weight of it stooping her aging back. Rafter lights spilled from the barn doors and Davey saw an arm fall from the canvas-wrapped parcel. He smiled.

"She got someone!"

Both children grinned and settled in their beds, eyes fixed to the ceiling. This was family growth.

Gratitude

Thank you to the following for help, inspiration, and/or support regarding the creation of this book: My wife, Mary, Mom & Dad Lutzke, Pete Kahle, John Boden, Dallas Mayr/AKA Jack Ketchum, Duncan Ralston, Nev Murray, Mark Matthews, Zach Bohannon, Amber Fallon, Todd Keisling, Jasper Bark, Michelle Garza and Melissa Lason (The Sisters of Slaughter), Bobby Dabicci, and Tim Meyer.

There is a lengthy list of readers who keep me writing by happily reading every book I write and helping spread the word. You know who you are. What you don't know is how much that means to me.

A special thank you to artist Robert Johnson who blessed me with the use of his beautiful artwork for the cover.

An extra special thank you to Abigail Brown, Madison Nischan, and Erin Varner who did much more than school me on what goes on behind the curtain in a funeral home, but showed me there's a whole other side to their work. Something that comes straight from their heart. Their empathy and compassion for the grieving and their respect for the dead helped create Emmett's character. Without them, this would be a different book.

About the Author

Chad has written for Famous Monsters of Filmland, Rue Morgue, Cemetery Dance, and Scream magazine. He's had dozens of short stories published, and some of his books include: OF FOSTER HOMES & FLIES, STIRRING THE SHEETS, SKULLFACE BOY, THE SAME DEEP WATER AS YOU, THE PALE WHITE, THE NEON OWL and WORMWOOD co-written with Tim Meyer. Lutzke's work has been praised by authors Jack Ketchum, Richard Chizmar, Joe Lansdale, Stephen Graham Jones, Elizabeth Massie and his own mother. He can be found lurking the internet at www.chadlutzke.com

Printed in Great Britain
by Amazon